Maurice M

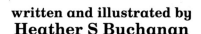

written and illustrated by
Heather S Buchanan

edited by Nina Filipek
designed by Liz Auger

Copyright © 1995 Heather S Buchanan. All rights reserved.
Published in Great Britain by World International,
an imprint of Egmont Publishing Ltd., Egmont House, PO Box 111,
Great Ducie Street, Manchester M60 3BL.
Printed in Finland. ISBN 0 7498 2278 3

A catalogue record for this book is available from the British Library.

Basil Bat's branch

N
W E
S

Rumpus Rabbit's burrow

Muzzy Mouse's house

Maurice Mole's hole

Scampa Squirrel's tree

Henrietta Hedgehog's log

Buttercup Meadow stretches from the Deep Dark Wood in the north, where Basil Bat and Scampa Squirrel live, to the small stream in the south, where Maurice Mole has his home.

Henrietta Hedgehog lives in an old log on the east side, and Muzzy Mouse's straw house is under the hedge to the west. In the middle of the meadow lives Rumpus Rabbit.

This is Maurice's story...

The animals were worried because their friend Maurice Mole had not been seen for days. Then Scampa Squirrel spotted a trail of molehills, stretching out across Buttercup Meadow. They knew Maurice liked to make new tunnels sometimes, but if only he would let them know when he was going on an expedition.

Underneath Buttercup Meadow, Maurice was digging away happily with his compass round his neck, and his map beside him. He was heading due South. By tomorrow, he expected to reach the stream where his old friend Water Vole lived, whom he hadn't seen for ages. He hoped Water Vole's larder was full of food because he had no way of letting him know he was coming. And, with all this digging, the mole was feeling very hungry indeed!

L ater on, Rumpus Rabbit was sitting sadly in his burrow, watching the rain beating down outside. The grass was too wet for running on, and the stream was rushing too fast through Buttercup Meadow for Rumpus to try to sail his raft. He tidied and swept the burrow, then wondered what else to do. He thought of Maurice Mole having an adventure, but keeping warm and dry at the same time. Rumpus thought it would be fun to dig his own tunnel, and meet up with the mole.

The rabbit began to dig. He dug for hours and hours. Soon a huge pile of soil built up behind him as the tunnel stretched further and further, and grew deeper and darker.

At last Rumpus began to feel very tired, so he lent his spade against the wall and sat down. But as he mopped his dusty whiskers with his handkerchief, he noticed what seemed to be a glint of gold! It was the edge of something large and round...

Rumpus tugged and pulled at the gold metal but it wouldn't come out of the earth. The only thing to do was to carry on and find Maurice Mole, and ask him to help. The rabbit left his handkerchief beside the treasure, to mark the spot, and started digging again as fast as he could. He forgot how tired he was, and certainly didn't stop to think what time it might be.

"I'm rich. I'm rich!" he said to himself with excitement.

Maurice Mole was peering up at the sky from one of his molehills. When he saw the stars twinkling away in the velvety darkness he knew it was time for him to sleep. He put down his spade, took off his compass, and settled down with his map covering him like a blanket. He was soon dreaming of the food awaiting him at Water Vole's house as he snuggled up next to the warm earth.

Early next morning, in his little waterfront home, Water Vole heard a terrible yelling and shouting. He ran out to his jetty and saw immediately what had happened. Rumpus had burrowed out into the stream, and the force of the water rushing in had picked him up and flung him straight through the wall of Maurice Mole's tunnel.

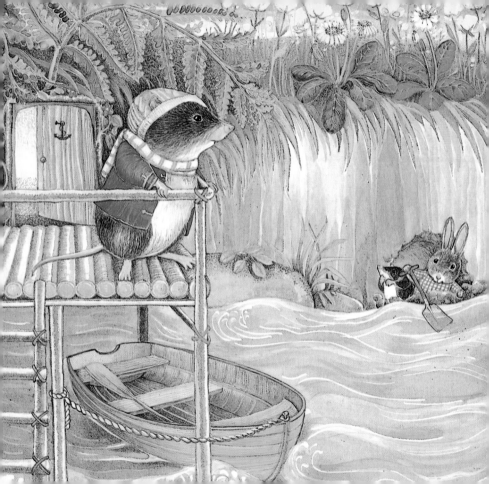

R umpus was amazed to find himself sitting on a very wet mole. And Maurice was equally amazed to be woken by the rabbit sitting on him – and his new tunnel flooded!

"Hello, Maurice," was all that Rumpus could think of to say. "I wanted to give you a surprise."

"You've certainly done that," said the mole, grabbing his compass and soggy map, just before they were washed away.

Luckily, Water Vole arrived in the nick of time, and they climbed into his boat for safety.

The little boat was swept along on the crest of a wave, deep into the tunnel. They travelled higher up the tunnel as they were carried back towards Rumpus's burrow. At last they bumped to a halt against some large stones, and Rumpus caught sight of his handkerchief – still pushed into the wall where he had left it.

"That's lucky!" he shouted. "This is the place where I found some buried treasure on the way to meet Maurice. Come and have a look."

Rumpus showed Maurice and Water Vole the thin edge of gold that glinted through the soil. The three animals pulled and heaved, and grunted and groaned, and in the end it did come free. But to Rumpus's bitter disappointment it was not a gold coin. It was an old pair of gold-coloured spectacles. Surprisingly, Maurice began to get very excited.

Maurice carried the spectacles to the entrance of Rumpus's burrow. He knocked out the glass lenses with his spade, and gave them to Water Vole to load into the boat. "These will make good port-hole windows for your house," said Maurice Mole. Then the mole sent Rumpus to fetch some soap, which he rubbed round one of the openings in the frame, whilst he held the other end in his strong paws.

The animals dipped the frame in a puddle of rainwater. Then Maurice held it up and told them to take a deep breath.

"Now, blow," said the mole.

To the amazement of Rumpus and Water Vole, an enormous shining bubble hovered there for a few moments before floating away.

"Oooh," they all sighed, not wanting the bubble to go.

The bubble sailed high up into the sky above Buttercup Meadow, and away over the trees of the Deep Dark Wood where it disappeared.

"Every cloud has a silver lining," smiled Maurice. He knew that Rumpus's terrible accident had actually done some good.

The spectacles Rumpus found could become the mole's signalling machine. Whenever he decided to go tunnelling he would send a bubble signal across the meadow. "Then you can all make sure you have food ready, in case I pay you a visit," he laughed.

As for Rumpus, he decided not to dig again. "There are some things better left to the experts!" he said. Everyone was relieved to hear that – especially Maurice!